W9-CCF-915

Written by Karen Lynn Williams **Illustrated by Linda Saport**

Eerdmans Books for Young Readers
Grand Rapids, Michigan • Cambridge, U.K.

Published 2005 by Eerdmans Books for Young Readers
An imprint of Wm. B. Eerdmans Publishing Company
255 Jefferson S.E., Grand Rapids, Michigan 49503
P.O. Box 163, Cambridge CB3 9PU U.K.

Printed and bound in China
05 06 07 08 09 10 7 6 5 4 3 2 1
ISBN 0-8028-5276-9
Library of Congress Cataloging-in-Publication Data

Williams, Karen Lynn.
Circles of hope / written by Karen Lynn Williams ; illustrated by Linda Saport.-- 1st ed.
p. cm.
Summary: After many futile attempts to plant a tree in honor of his new baby sister, a young Haitian boy discovers the perfect solution.
ISBN 0-8028-5276-9 (alk. paper)
[1. Trees--Planting--Fiction. 2. Babies--Fiction. 3. Haiti--Fiction.] I. Saport, Linda, ill. II. Title.
PZ7.W66655Ci 2005
[E]--dc22
2004006801

The illustrations were rendered in charcoal and pastel on paper.
The display type was set in Urbana.
The text type was set in Helvetica Neue.
Art Director Gayle Brown
Graphic Design Matthew Van Zomeren

In memory of Gwen Grant Mellon for the hope she brought to Deschapelles and Haiti and the remarkable example she set for those of us who knew her. —K.L.W.

In memory of Tux. —L.S.

Everyone brought a gift for baby Lucía. Facile sat high up in his mango tree and watched. It was the only tree on the whole dusty mountaintop. Papa had planted it for him when he was born. “A strong tree protects its timoun,” Papa said. Now Papa worked far away in the city.

Facile had no gift for his baby sister. No tikado at all. He ate a juicy sweet mango, licked his sticky fingers, and thought, “Papa is not here to plant a tree for baby Lucía.” He studied the large white pit of the mango and knew what his gift would be.

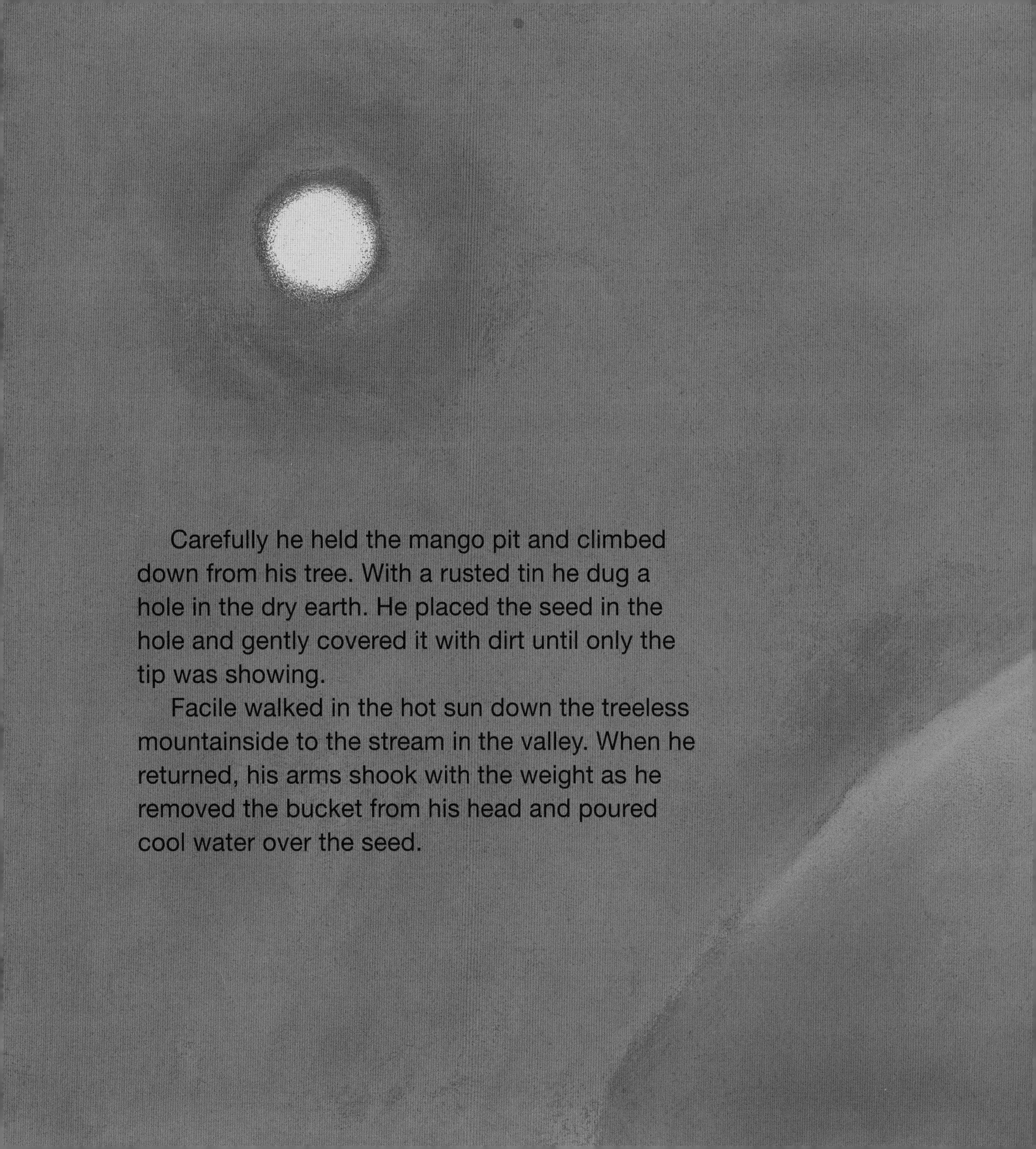

Carefully he held the mango pit and climbed down from his tree. With a rusted tin he dug a hole in the dry earth. He placed the seed in the hole and gently covered it with dirt until only the tip was showing.

Facile walked in the hot sun down the treeless mountainside to the stream in the valley. When he returned, his arms shook with the weight as he removed the bucket from his head and poured cool water over the seed.

After many days, the seed began to sprout. But when Facile came up the mountain with water, he found only an empty hole and the neighbor's goat blinking stupidly. "Look what you have done." Facile shook his fist. Once again he had not even a small gift for his new sister.

“How can I plant a tree that will grow strong?” Facile asked cousin Solvab.

“You must make a fence of cactus,” his cousin told him. And so Facile planted another seed, and this time he protected it with stalks from the kandélab.

Dark gray clouds piled up behind the mountains. An early rain came crashing down on the dusty mountaintop. Facile danced in the puddles. Lucía laughed. But when he went to check on his sister's tree, Facile could not believe his eyes. "Gone," he cried. There was only a piece of cactus fence and beyond that the lifeless seed.

Facile asked Mama, "How can I plant a tree that will grow strong?"

But Mama was worried about Lucía, who was very hot. Lucía was not eating, and she did not laugh at Facile's games. "I must take Lucía to the doctor in the city. You will stay with Tonton." Then before she carried his sister down the mountain, Mama said, "You must make a step to plant Lucía's tree."

Facile dug a flat step in the mountainside so the rain could not steal his seed. Again, Lucía's tree began to sprout. Facile waited, but Mama and Lucía did not return.

Then one day the men in the village made scrub fires to clear the land for planting. At night the sparkling flames crisscrossed the mountain. The smoke stung Facile's eyes.

The next day Facile saw ashes as he walked through the yard, and when he got to his step he cried, “Ah, non!” Lucía’s tiny tree had turned into a black twisted stick. Lucía had been away for many weeks, and Facile still had no small gift for his sister.

Facile helped Tonton to clear the many white stones from their garden. He watched the path for Mama and Lucía, but they did not come. "I cannot plant a tree that will grow strong for Lucía," Facile told Tonton.

"Éspéré," Tonton said. "You must have hope to plant a tree."

Facile sighed and shook his head. "Too many stones." Stones did not make a gift, and stones did not protect a timoun. He tossed another stone from the garden into the pile, and then he had an idea.

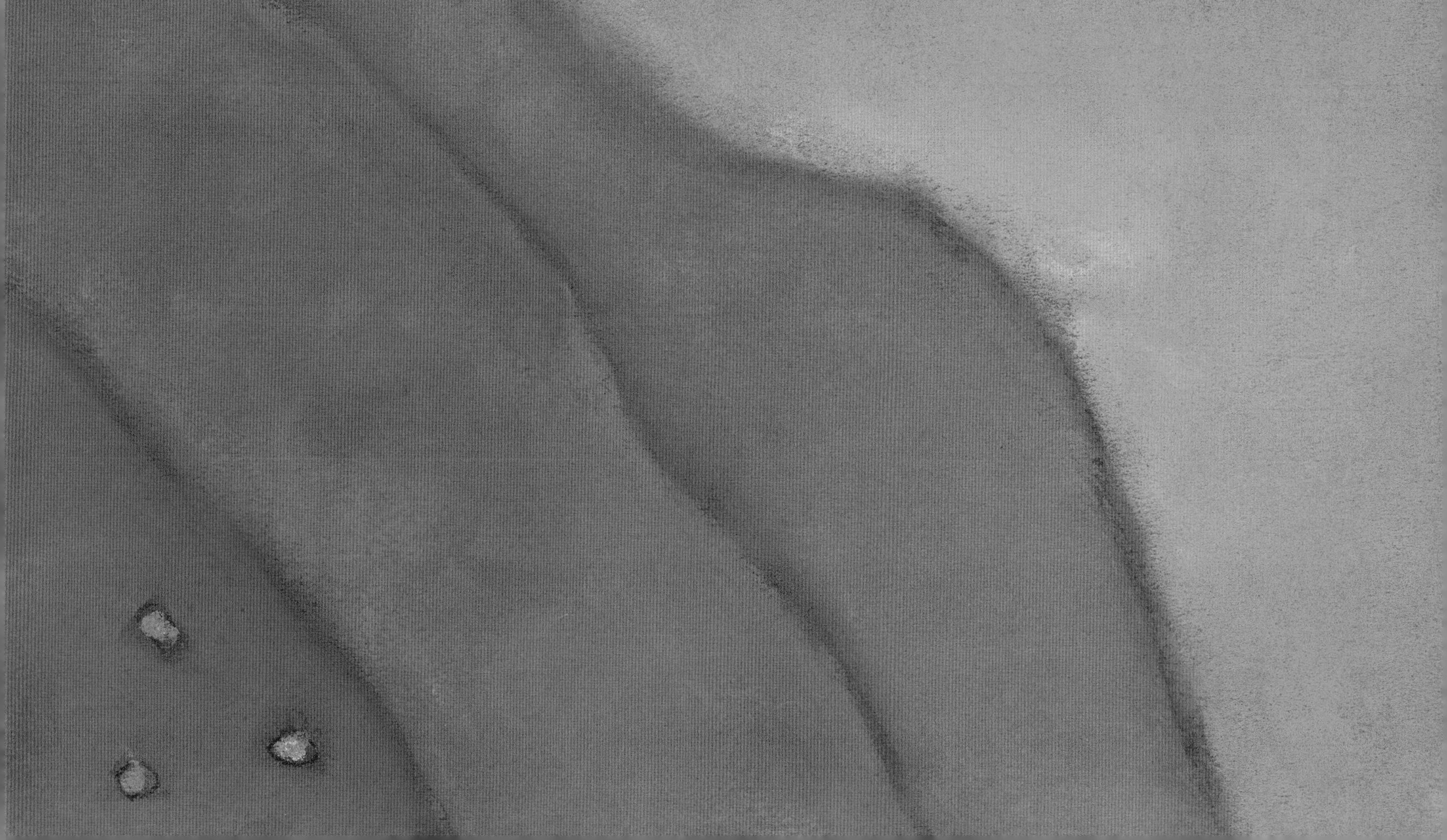

One after another he piled the stones up. Up and around he built the wall. When he was done the circle of stones was nearly as high as his waist.

Facile began to have hope. He climbed inside the wall and scraped a hole in the hard earth. One more time he planted a seed for Lucía.

He carried water and watched and waited, and finally Lucía's tree began to grow inside the circle. It changed from a tiny sprout to a large brown twig with leaves.

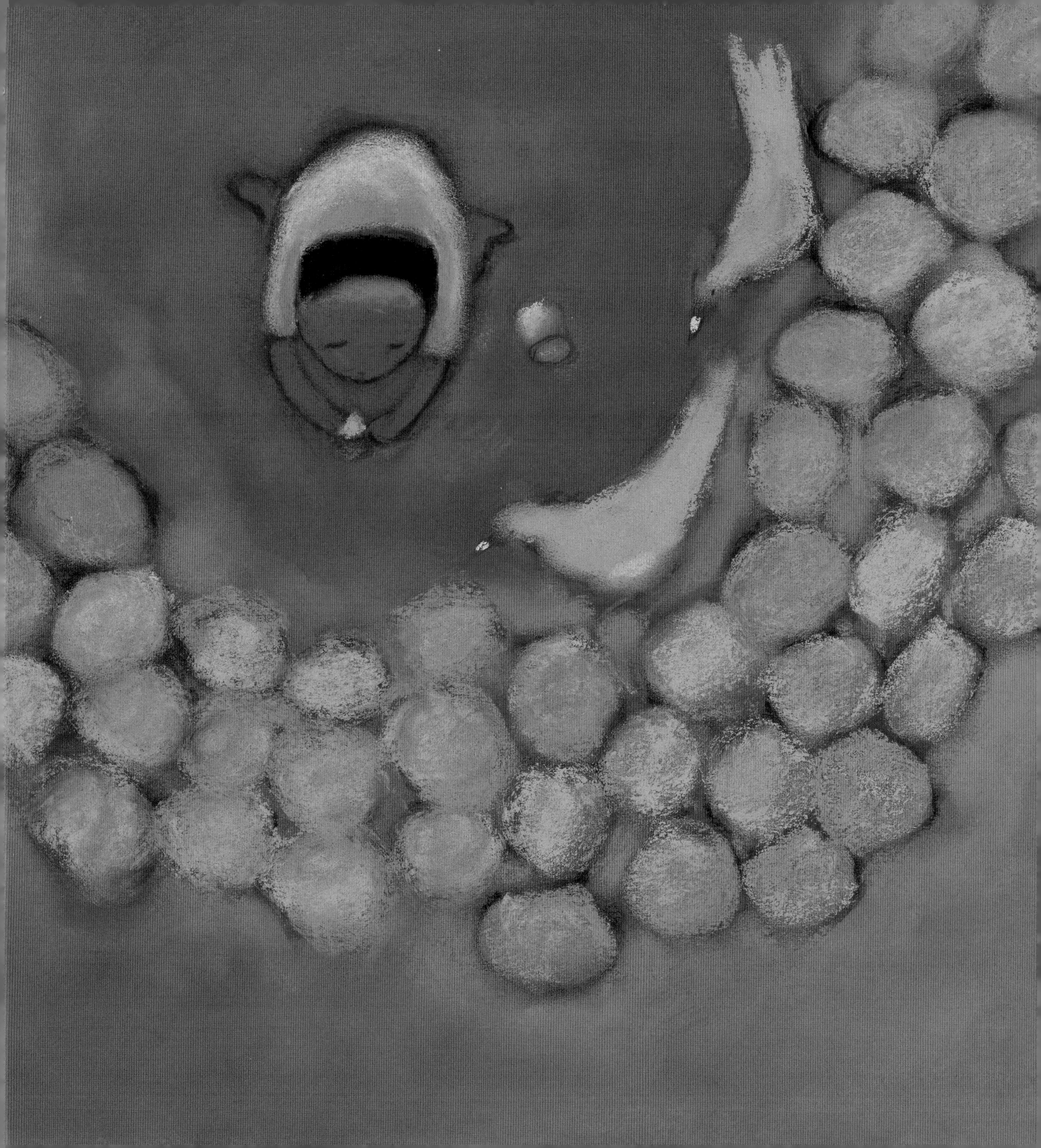

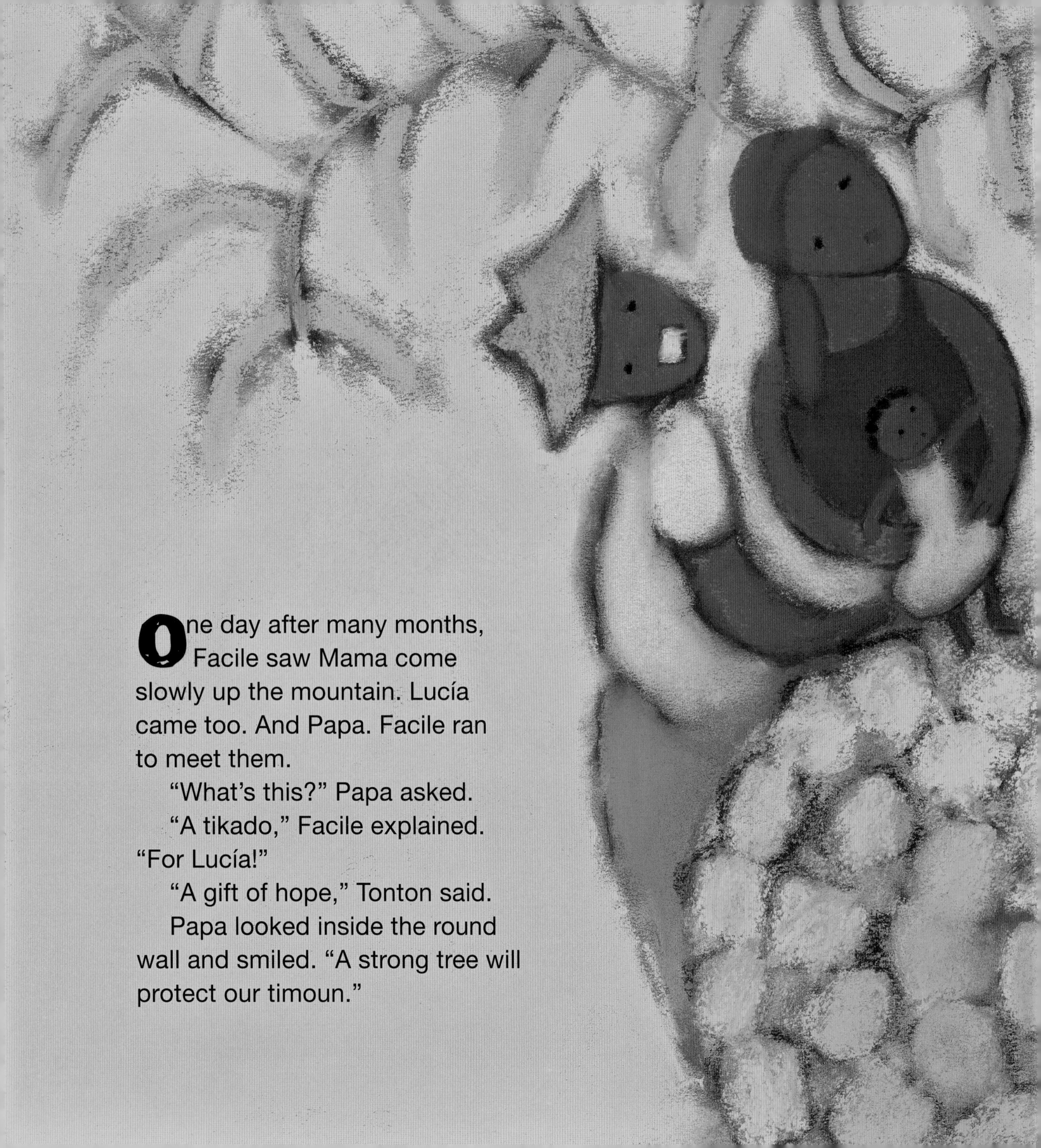

One day after many months, Facile saw Mama come slowly up the mountain. Lucía came too. And Papa. Facile ran to meet them.

"What's this?" Papa asked.

"A tikado," Facile explained. "For Lucía!"

"A gift of hope," Tonton said.

Papa looked inside the round wall and smiled. "A strong tree will protect our timoun."

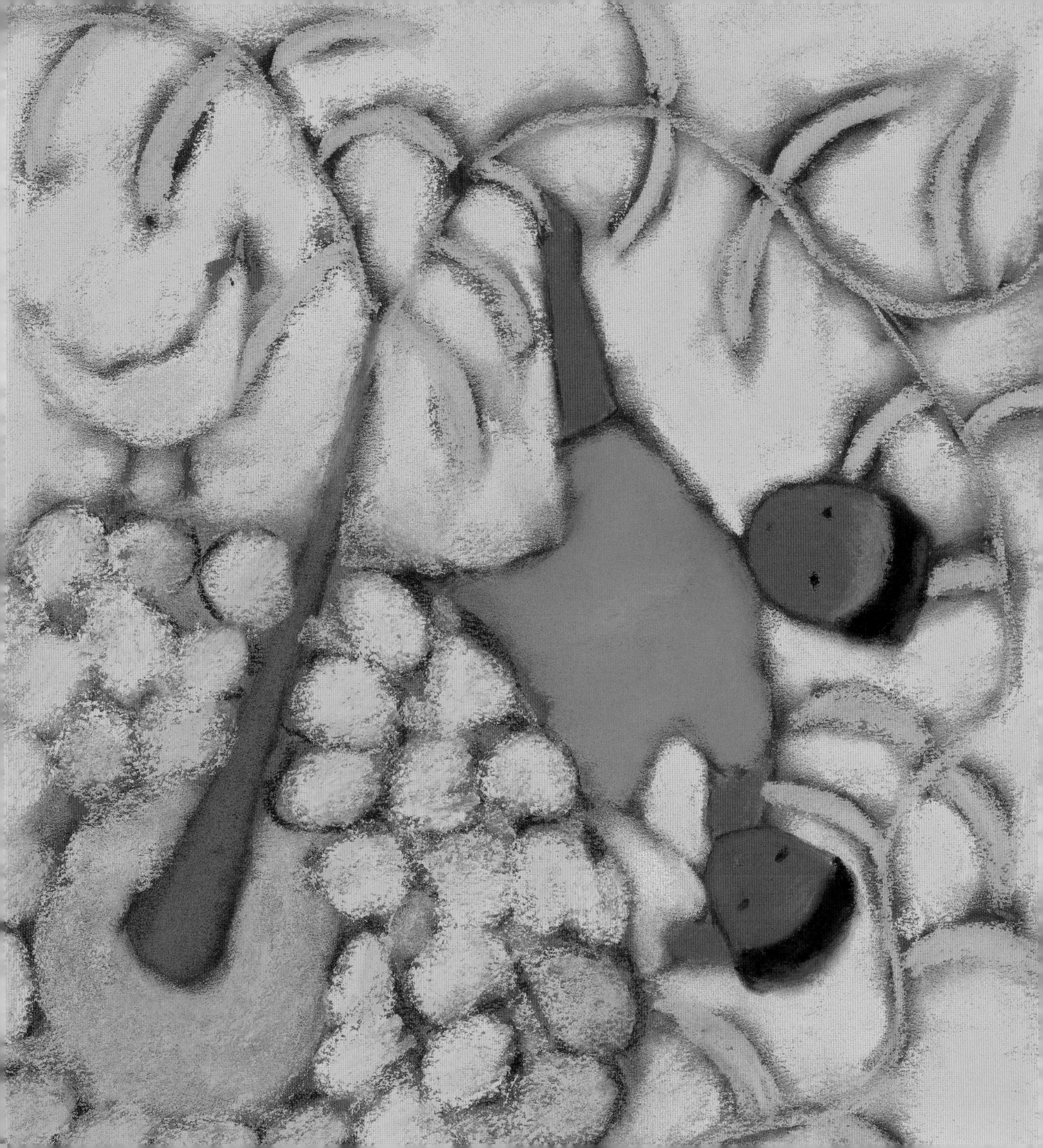

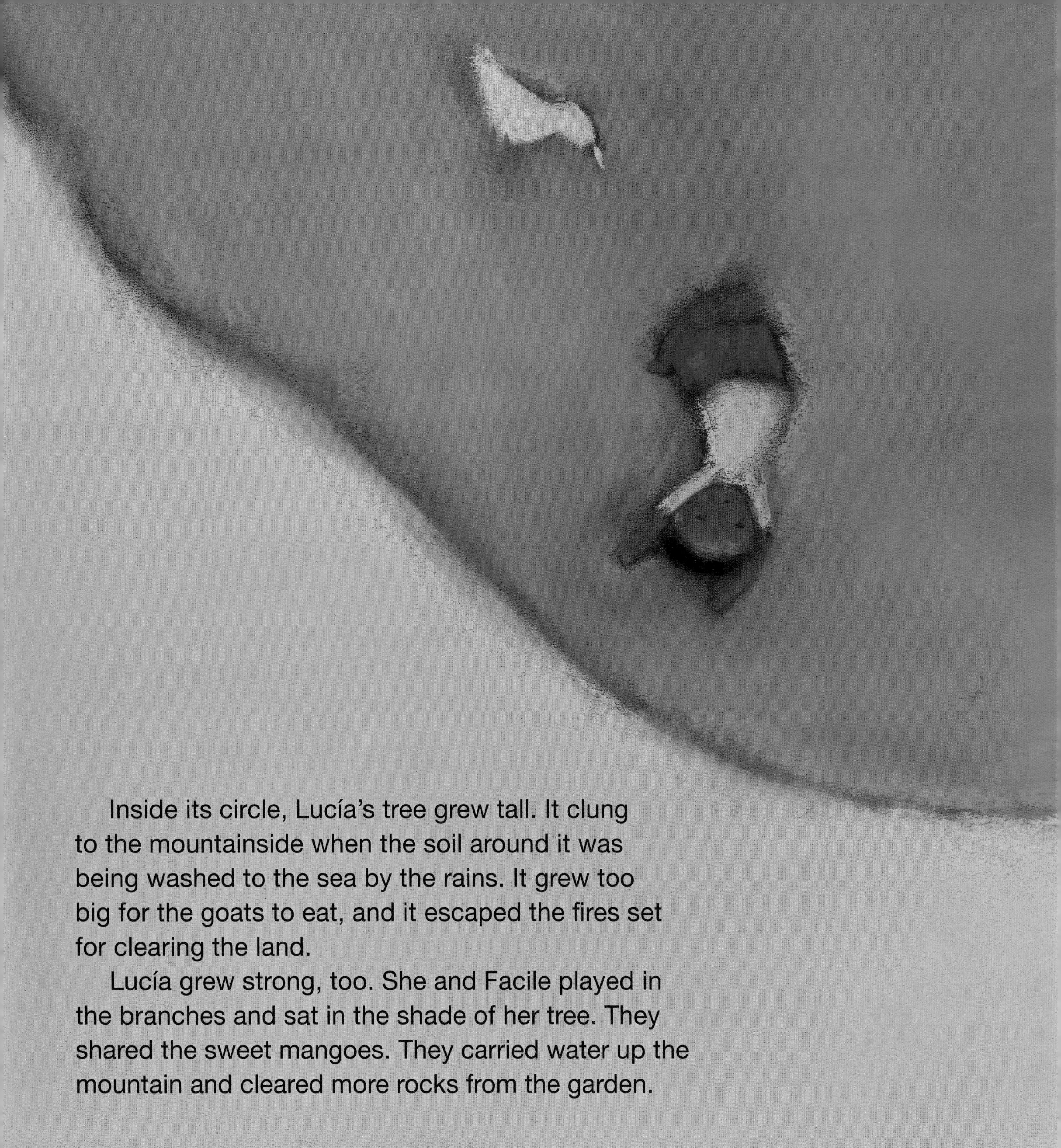

Inside its circle, Lucía's tree grew tall. It clung to the mountainside when the soil around it was being washed to the sea by the rains. It grew too big for the goats to eat, and it escaped the fires set for clearing the land.

Lucía grew strong, too. She and Facile played in the branches and sat in the shade of her tree. They shared the sweet mangoes. They carried water up the mountain and cleared more rocks from the garden.

And slowly, one year at a time, little circles of hope began to grow on the mountainsides of Haiti, and inside each circle grew a tree.

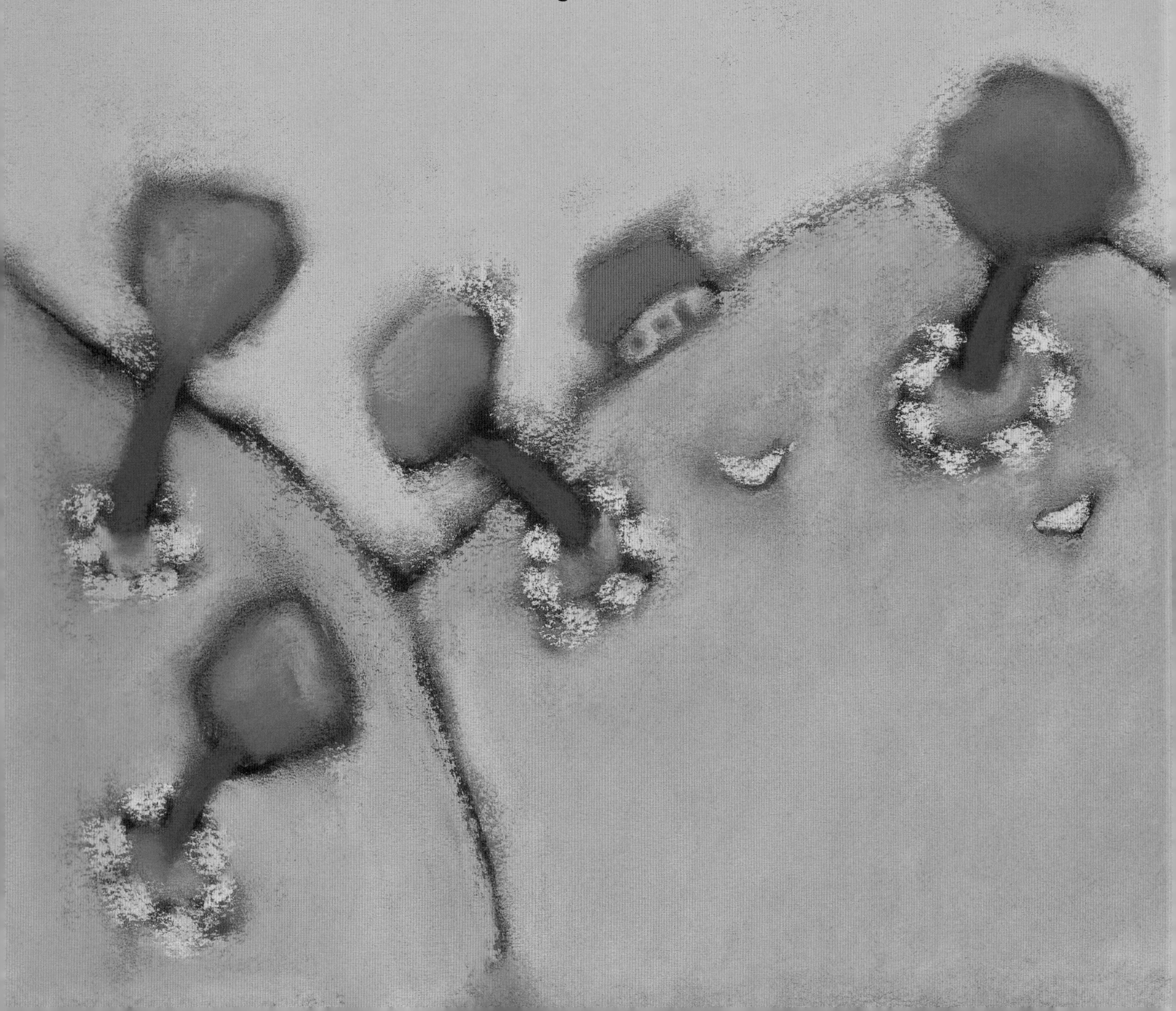

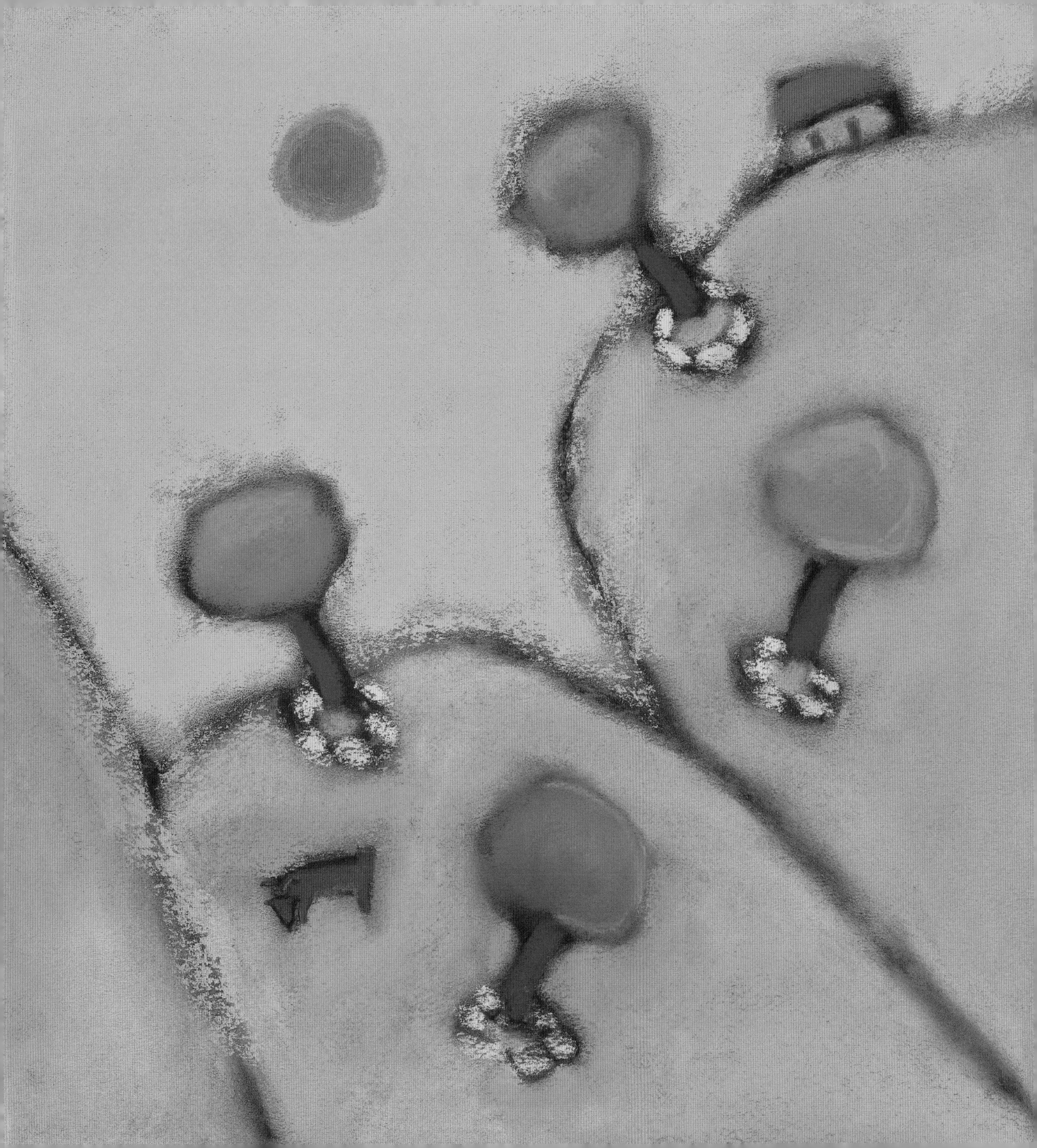

Glossary

The language spoken by most of the people in rural Haiti is called Haitian Creole (Kréyól). It combines elements of several African languages and French.

Ah, non—oh, no

Bon—good

Éspéré—hope

Kandélab—a type of cactus that branches out like a candelabra and is used in Haiti to make fences

Tikado—small gift

Timoun—child, children

Tonton—uncle or grandfather

Author's Note

Haiti shares a small island in the Caribbean with the Dominican Republic. It is a land of many mountains. Long ago Haiti was a rich French colony known for its lush green countryside. It was called "The Jewel of the Antilles." Then the Haitian slaves successfully fought the French for their independence and began a long struggle to live off the land.

Trees have always been very important to the Haitian people. Traditionally, when a child was born the child's umbilical cord was planted in the earth along with the seed of a fruit tree. The tree that grew from that seed was seen as a guardian of the child. ("A strong tree protects its timoun.") Over the years, however, many trees in Haiti have been cut down for lumber and to make charcoal for cooking fires. This has left the mountainsides brown and bare and vulnerable to soil erosion when it rains.

Today in Haiti small groups of people are working to plant trees again on the mountainsides. It is difficult, because so much soil has already eroded and the people still struggle to find enough wood to meet their needs. But with hard work, patience, and new methods of planting and protecting young trees, progress is being made. A few rural mountainsides are now dotted with circular stone walls, and inside each stone circle grows a tree of hope for the future.